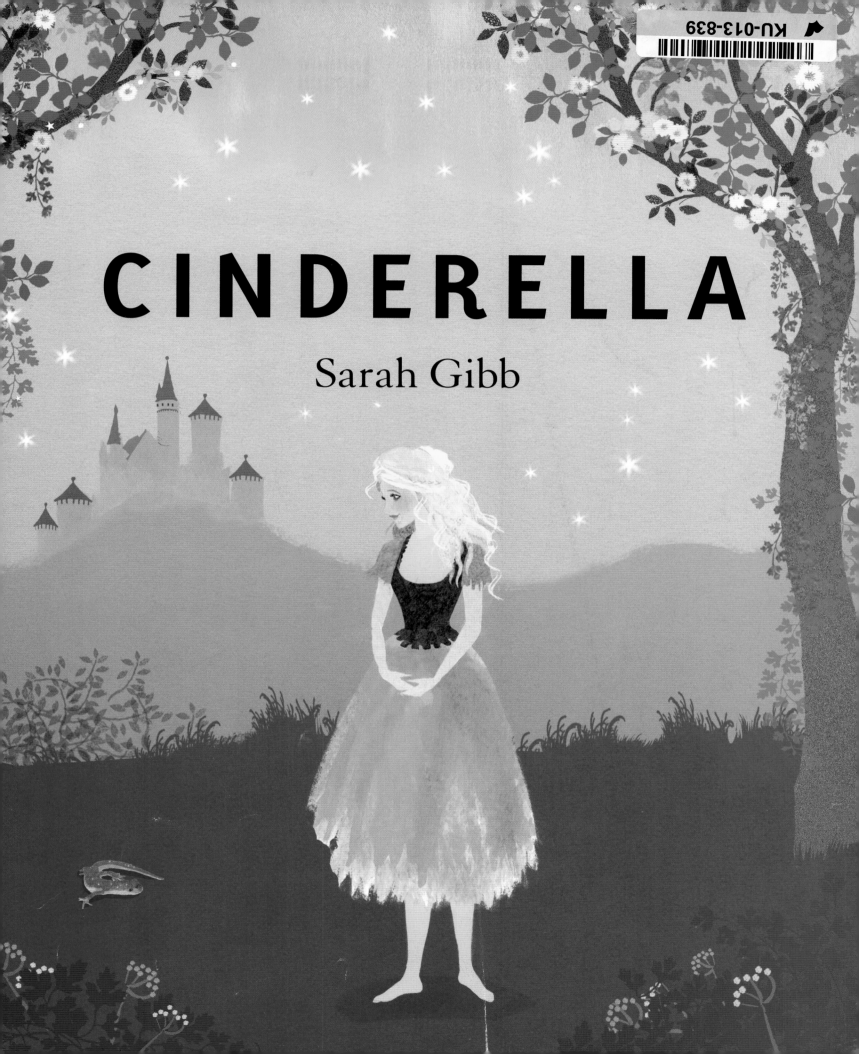

CINDERELLA

Sarah Gibb

KU-013-839

THIS BOOK BELONGS TO

....

....

First published in hardback in Great Britain by
HarperCollins Children's Books in 2016

3 5 7 9 10 8 6 4 2

ISBN: 978-0-00-817188-9

HarperCollins Children's Books is a division of HarperCollins Publishers Ltd.

Text by Alison Sage
Text copyright © HarperCollins Publishers Ltd 2016
Illustrations copyright © Sarah Gibb 2016

The illustrator asserts the moral right to be identified as the illustrator of the work.
A CIP catalogue record for this title is available from the British Library. All rights reserved.
No part of this publication may be reproduced, stored in a retrieval system or transmitted
in any form or by any means, electronic, mechanical, photocopying, recording or otherwise,
without the prior permission of HarperCollins Publishers Ltd,
1 London Bridge Street, London SE1 9GF.

Visit our website at www.harpercollins.co.uk

Printed in China

HarperCollins *Children's Books*

Once, a long time ago, there lived a girl called Ella. She was as sunny as a summer breeze, and as gorgeous as a field of lilies. Her mother had died when she was a baby, and after many years of living alone, her father married again. Ella's stepmother was pretty to look at, but she was cruel and her two daughters were as unkind as she was.

Doris, the elder, was as silly as she was spiteful. Jezebel, the younger girl, was clever but she was never happier than when she was finding fault with other people.

Both sisters hated Ella from the moment they met.

"Nasty little creep," said Doris. "She shan't have any of *my* clothes." For her mother gave both daughters anything they wanted, while Ella soon had to make do with old rags.

"Little beast," said Jezebel. "Make her sleep in the kitchen."

And that is what happened. Poor Ella was sent to the cold kitchen where she curled up in the cinders to keep warm.

"Look at Cinder-ella!" sneered Jezebel. "She is just where she belongs."

The name stuck and it was "Cinderella, fetch this!" and "Cinderella, clear that away!" all day long. As the months passed, the two sisters grew more mean and spoiled, but Cinderella was as warm-hearted as ever.

One morning, a letter arrived from the palace. The King was holding a grand ball for the prince to choose a wife. Any girl who thought she could catch his eye was invited. Doris and Jezebel were overcome with excitement. What luck! Each felt sure that she was going to be the one the prince would choose.

"He'll dance with me all night," daydreamed Doris. "I'll be in my pink silk with the cream ruffles."

"You'll look like a raspberry pudding!" jeered Jezebel. "He'll be dancing with *me* in my elegant yellow satin with the black lace…"

As Cinderella listened to her stepsisters, a tear rolled down her cheek. If only she could go to the ball too! But that was impossible. She was ragged little Cinderella with nothing grand to wear.

What a fuss and flurry followed over the next few days as Jezebel and Doris dithered over what to wear. Cinderella had no peace from morning until night, helping them to squeeze into one hideous outfit after another.

On the evening of the ball the stepsisters were ready at last.

"Don't forget to tidy up while we're gone!" ordered Doris as their carriage swept away down the drive.

Cinderella slipped back to her place in the cinders and cried her heart out. "I wish I could see the prince!" she sobbed.

All of a sudden, she heard someone calling her name.

"Cinderella! Do stop crying, dear. I'm your fairy godmother."

At Cinderella's side was a beautiful and elegant lady.

"I *wish* I could go to the ball," Cinderella whispered through her tears.

"Then go you shall," said her fairy godmother, smiling as she took out a wand made of stars. "Get me a pumpkin from the garden. A nice big one."

Cinderella was so surprised that she did as she was told.

"Now I need four little brown mice," said her strange visitor. "Oh – and a fat frog, if you can find one. And two lizards."

When Cinderella had brought everything her godmother waved her wand and…

Pouff! In a flash of white light a magnificent golden coach appeared with four beautiful horses and a fine coachman. Two footmen leapt smartly up to their places at the back.

"Oh!" cried Cinderella joyfully. But then her face fell. "What about my dress?"

"Hold still, my dear." Again her godmother waved her wand in a sparkle of fairy dust.

Cinderella gasped. She was wearing a dress of the purest gold. It glittered in the darkness as if the sun had come out, and Cinderella blinked at its brilliance. Her hair was twined with snowdrops and pearls, and on her feet were the most beautiful golden slippers.

Cinderella's godmother laughed at her amazed face. "Off you go!" she said kindly. "But listen. My spell will only last until midnight. As soon as the clock strikes, all your finery will turn back to rags, so be sure to get home by then."

"I promise," said Cinderella and she sprang into the coach and whirled away to the palace.

When Cinderella arrived, the ball was already in full swing and she could hear the sound of music and the happy chatter of the dancers.

She pushed open the great doors and walked into the hall.

There was a gasp of admiration as everyone saw her. The prince, who had been sitting next to his father, leapt to his feet and crossed the hall to take her hand.

Bowing, the prince asked her to dance and as they swept down the long hall he could not take his eyes off her.

"Who can she be?" whispered the ladies.

"She must be a fairy princess," said the courtiers.

Cinderella had never been so happy. The evening passed in a brilliant blur of laughter and loveliness, the prince always at her side. She spoke kindly to her stepsisters, who didn't recognise her. They blushed with joy to be noticed by the unknown princess.

Cinderella watched the great clock in the hall, counting each precious minute of her time with the prince. She dared not stay too long. At half past eleven, she gave the prince one last smile and slipped away before he realised what was happening.

She ran out of the hall, down the steps and into her coach. And she was gone, leaving the prince desperately searching for her amongst the groups of dancers.

At midnight Cinderella slipped into her old place in the cinders and just as she did so, her dress turned into rags. Four squeaking mice raced across the floor and she knew that her coach was now nothing but a large orange pumpkin.

Soon after, the key rattled in the lock and her stepsisters returned, pink-faced and excited at the wonderful happenings at the ball.

"We made friends with a mystery princess," said Doris. "She came and talked to us."

"Is that so?" murmured Cinderella.

"Yes, I shouldn't wonder if the prince doesn't talk to us next," said Jezebel. "There's going to be another ball tomorrow night. The King has invited everyone again."

"Can I come?" asked Cinderella daringly.

"Don't be stupid," said Doris.

The next evening, the sisters got ready as before. As the unknown princess had worn a golden dress, they both chose golden dresses too.

Jezebel's sour little face poked out from her gold jewellery like a disagreeable bird. Doris' cheeks shone like lard under a layer of powder.

"Have a good time," called Cinderella as they set off.

Once again her fairy godmother was there, but this time Cinderella was not weeping. She clapped her hands with delight as her coach magically appeared and, at the touch of a wand, her rags disappeared. They became the most beautiful shell-pink dress, as fine as cobwebs and shimmering with light. Her little shoes were mother-of-pearl and her hair was twined with rosebuds.

Full of thanks, Cinderella sped off to the ball a second time.

"Don't forget to be back before twelve!" called her fairy godmother.

Just as before, the ball had already begun, but the moment she entered the hall, the music stopped. The prince's face, which had been downcast, broke into a wonderful smile and he hurried across the hall to lead her in the next dance.

They talked and talked and afterwards all Cinderella could remember was that they had agreed about everything. They stood quietly watching the dancers when suddenly Cinderella glanced up at the clock. It was quarter to twelve!

She slipped out of the hall, jumped into her coach and away she flew. As the coach was coming up the road towards her house, the clock struck twelve and suddenly she was running home through the darkness in her old rags.

Before long, her sisters came back, chattering excitedly about the ball.

"Was the princess there again tonight?" Cinderella asked them.

"Yes," frowned Jezebel. "And the prince wanted to dance with no one but her."

"But then she disappeared again before he could ask who she was," said Doris, "so everyone is going to another ball tomorrow."

"And we shall wear pink next, so you'd better start getting our things ready," snarled Jezebel.

On the third night, everything happened as before, except that this time, Cinderella's dress was sky blue silk, scattered with diamonds and opals which flickered like little flames as she moved. On her feet was the most exquisite pair of glass slippers. She looked like a queen.

The prince was waiting for her by the door and the moment she arrived they whirled into a dance.

Then the prince took her hand, and they stood gazing into each other's eyes. Time seemed to stand still and then all of a sudden, Cinderella heard the big clock beginning to strike…

Midnight! She flew from the prince's arms like a startled deer, out of the ballroom and down the great wide steps just as the chimes were finishing. As she ran she dropped one of her little glass slippers.

No one noticed as a girl in rags slipped out of the palace gates and down the road.

Cinderella barely had time to race through the door and sit by the cinders before her stepsisters arrived home.

"What have you been up to?" said Jezebel suspiciously.

"Nothing," yawned Cinderella. "Tell me about the princess!"

"You'll never believe it!" said Doris. "She disappeared *again*."

"She dropped a glass slipper," broke in Jezebel, "and the King says that whoever it fits will marry the prince."

The next day, messengers went out to every corner of the kingdom, north, east, south and west, spreading the news. Whoever the shoe fitted would be the royal bride.

"It could be me!" said Doris.

"You!" said Jezebel scornfully. "That slipper is going to fit *me*!" And she rubbed her feet with cream to make them smooth and slippery.

Soon the prince arrived.

He hoped that the slipper would not fit either of the sisters, but he offered it to them politely.

They tried… and tried. But the harder they pushed, the more their feet bulged out of the little shoe.

"Have you any sisters?" asked the prince.

"Only Cinders," said Doris spitefully, "but she doesn't wear shoes at all!"

"Let her try," said the prince.

So they called for Cinderella who sat down shyly and picked up the little glass slipper.

It fitted perfectly.

And then she put her hand in her pocket and pulled out the other slipper and put that on too.

Doris was too amazed to say a word.

"There must be some mistake!" gasped Jezebel.

"There's no mistake," smiled the fairy godmother, appearing at that moment. "This is your princess," she said to the prince.

"Yes, I know," he replied, because even in her rags he knew that she was the one.

Cinderella and her prince were married straight away and everyone said that there had never been a lovelier princess, or a more handsome prince.

Cinderella invited all of her family to the wedding and her stepsisters danced with the greatest lords of the land. Her fairy godmother showered Cinderella and the prince with fairy dust, but they hardly noticed because each already had their heart's desire.

Cinderella never forgot her days in rags, and she always had a kind word for everyone, rich or poor. She also could never find it in her heart to chase the mice out of the palace kitchens, or the frogs from the royal pond.

In time, she and her prince became King and Queen and ruled their country wisely and well, but their happiness never faded, and nor did their undying love.